Monster Boy's Field Trip

BY CARL EMERSON
ILLUSTRATED BY LON LEVIN

visit us at www.abdopublishing.com

Published by Magic Wagon, a division of the ABDO Publishing Group, 8000 West 78th Street, Edina, Minnesota 55439. Copyright © 2009 by Abdo Consulting Group, Inc. International copyrights reserved in all countries. All rights reserved. No part of this book may be reproduced in any form without written permission from the publisher.

Looking Glass Library™ is a trademark and logo of Magic Wagon.

Printed in the United States.

Text by Carl Emerson
Illustrations by Lon Levin
Edited by Patricia Stockland
Interior layout and design by Emily Love
Cover design by Emily Love

Library of Congress Cataloging-in-Publication Data

Emerson, Carl.
Monster Boy's field trip / by Carl Emerson ; illustrated by Lon Levin.
   p. cm. — (Monster Boy)
ISBN 978-1-60270-236-3
[1. Monsters—Fiction. 2. Zoos—Fiction.] I. Levin, Lon, ill. II. Title.
 PZ7.E582Mof 2008
 [E]– –dc22
                                   2008003654

Marty Onster handed a permission slip to his mom.

"We're going on a field trip next week," he said proudly.

Mrs. Onster was not sure she wanted Marty to go on a field trip. After all, if he went to a museum or some other normal place, he might just become even more human.

Later that week, she looked at the slip. "The zoo!" she exclaimed. "The zoo will be a great place for you to practice your growling!"

Marty sighed. He didn't want to practice his growling in front of his friends. He saved that for home, when only monsters were around.

A week later, Marty and his classmates got on a bus to go to the zoo. Marty sat next to his best friend, Sally Weet.

"I can't wait to get to the zoo!" Sally said. "We are going to see penguins and zebras and monkeys!"

Unfortunately, Bart Ully sat down in the seat across from Marty.

"Yeah, and we are going to see sharks and bats and snakes, too," Bart said to Sally. "Your favorites are all the wimpy animals. Hey Onster, what's your favorite?"

"I like them all," Marty said.

"You probably like them because you are one of them," Bart snapped. "A creature."

"We are all creatures," Marty shot back. "Some of us are just a little more creature-y than others."

Before they knew it, they were at the zoo. Sally wanted to see all the different birds. So, Marty and Sally went to the aviary first.

They walked in the door and looked at the macaws and other colorful birds. When the birds saw Marty, they all started screeching and flew away.

"Get away! Warning! It's a monster!" Marty heard someone say.

"Did you hear that?" Marty asked a confused Sally.

"Yeah," Sally said. "They were all screeching like crazy."

"No, I mean, did you hear someone say something?" Marty asked.

"All I heard was the birds," Sally replied. "We must have scared them."

When they got to the penguin area, the same thing happened. All the penguins stopped playing. They all dived, swam, and waddled away as fast as they could.

"Predator!" Marty heard someone say.

"Monster!" said someone else.

"Did you hear that?" Marty said to Sally.

"Yeah, I've never heard penguins make so much noise," Sally replied.

"No, I mean the words," Marty said. Sally shook her head.

Marty's day kept getting worse.

When the hippos ran away, Marty heard, "Help us! Help us!"

When the monkeys swung to the farthest branches,
Marty heard, "Head for the treetops!"

When the zebras stampeded away, Marty heard,
"Let's hoof it out of here!"

Finally, Marty decided to tell Sally the truth.

"I know what's happening," he said.
"They are all afraid of me."

"Afraid of you? Why?" Sally replied.
"You are super nice to animals."

"Sally, I'm a monster," he said.

"Oh, don't listen to that Bart Ully,"
Sally said. "He doesn't know
what he's talking about."

Sally started to walk toward the next exhibit.

"No, Sally," Marty said. "You don't understand. I'm really, well, I mean, my parents are really m—"

Before he could get the words out, Marty and Sally were standing in front of the shark tank. Suddenly, all of the sharks were swimming straight toward them!

"See?" Sally said. "They like you. You're not a monster, Marty. You just have a little bit of a temper, that's all."

Sally and Marty continued through the exhibits. At the bear enclosure, all the bears walked toward Marty and stared at him. Soon, all the kids gathered around Marty.

Finally, one of the bears flashed Marty a big, toothy grin. "Hey, buddy," it said. "Any of these kids worth eating? Think maybe you could help a guy out here?"

Marty jumped back. "Did you hear that?" Marty yelled.

"Yes," Sally said. "That was a loud growl all right. But it wasn't anything to get so scared about. He's behind a glass wall, after all."

Then, Marty remembered the growling lessons his parents had given him. He growled back and said, "Sorry. I can't help you. These kids are my friends."

Sally stared at Marty. Just then, Bart came up.

"Hey, check it out!" Bart bellowed. "Onster is talking to his friends! What's he, your brother or something?"

Marty's fur started rising on his back. He started huffing and puffing. He didn't want to turn into a monster in front of his friends. But before he could stop, he was covered in fur and drool.

"C'mon, dude," the bear said. "At least let me eat *that* one."

The rest of the children stared as Marty and the bear talked.
Marty quickly calmed down.

"Nah, I don't think you'd like that one,"
Marty growled back, smiling. "He's too sour."

Contain Your Inner Monster

Tips from Marty Onster

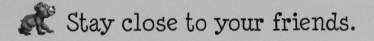

Walk away from a person or situation that is making you frustrated.

Stay close to your friends.

Talk to an adult about what you are feeling.

Remember, no matter how much you want to—do not eat people!